THE DANCING FAUN

The Dancing Faun

by
Florence
Farr

REBEL SATORI PRESS
New Orleans
2020

THE DANCING FAUN

'YES, Lady Geraldine, the only beauty in modern life is its falsehood. Its reality is ridiculous.'

'Truth always was undignified, Mr. Travers.' 'Just so; that is why the art of life consists in not realising the truth,' replied the man, with charming languor.

'You are the first person I have met who has dared put these things into words,' murmured the woman. 'Your life has been a dream hitherto.' 'According to you, I had better not awake." One wants experience to give a wider scope to one's dreams,' said he paternally.

'A woman's imagination has no such needs.'

'That depends. What are your favourite books?'

'I dislike reading. In novels, people always do

1

what you expect. The only tolerable people are those who do what you do not expect.'

'And this is your first season!'

'I have four elder sisters.'

'Ah!—' he paused, then he added, 'one never realises how much women tell each other.'

'No, in men's eyes, women are always at daggers drawn, fighting for the exclusive possession of a masculine heart.'

'Geraldine,' cried her mother, from the other end of the drawing-room, 'come and sing to us, my dear. Mr. Clausen has not heard your voice since your return from Paris.'

'Have you made a serious study of singing, Lady Geraldine?' asked Travers.

'I had a course of lessons from Sautussi in the winter.'

'Oh yes, Mr. Travers, indeed she has,' broke in Lady Kirkdale as she crossed the room; 'and I insisted on her singing at Sautussi's reception, just the same as the other pupils. I think it is the greatest mistake to make distinctions of rank in matters of art. In art all are equal. There is something so beautiful in that thought.' Lady Kirkdale pulled up the rose-coloured blind.

'Will you open the piano, Mr. Travers? I am sure you are devoted to music, you have the musical physiognomy.'

'Then I fear I have a very foolish physiognomy.'

'Now, now, don't be severe. Kirkdale tells me you are most delightfully severe, and say such witty things.'

'Then Lord Kirkdale has done me an infinite wrong: to have the reputation of a wit precede him is the ruin of a man.'

'I assure you, you are mistaken; most people are much too stupid to distinguish the qualities of wit; once establish a reputation, half the world takes you on trust, and considers the other half criticises you because it envies you.'

'You give me hope, Lady Kirkdale.'

'Mr. Travers, I am afraid you are a very, very bad man. Come, let us go to the piano.'

The Marchioness of Kirkdale had always been enterprising. She had the experience of life only given to those ladies whose husbands are thoroughly and brutally immoral: voluptuaries who have no foresight, who do not realise that it is sometimes amusing to talk to an innocent woman, when one is thoroughly bored by those who are not innocent.

Lady Kirkdale's suspicions had been aroused by the violent friendship her young son had conceived for George Travers; and having her own theories about the education of young men, she at once invited her son's crony to afternoon tea at the little house they occupied in Davies Street, Berkeley Square. 'A man's behaviour in a drawing-room is one of the tests you should always apply before you allow him to enjoy your confidence, Stephen,' she had said.

'A drawing-room is such an inconceivably uninteresting place,' sighed Stephen.

'That is the reason why, as a test, it is so invaluable; any commonly brilliant man can amuse men in a club, or women at the Continental; but it requires the most subtle quintessence of wit to penetrate the brain of the great world without shocking its susceptibilities; neither radical paradoxes nor coarse allusions can be brought into play there, without social ruin.'

'Is social ruin possible nowadays?'

'My dear Kirkdale!'

'I gauge the public feeling of society by

its attitude in public, and when I sit in a box at the theatre and see the stalls greet the passionate utterances of a ruined woman with a contemptuous smile, as if that sort of sentiment were quite out of date, I come to the conclusion that social ruin means nothing now.'

'My poor Kirkdale, if you think society is represented in the stalls at a theatre, you are still more unsophisticated than I had dared hope. But you and Geraldine are always puzzling me. There is a persistence of innocence, I might almost say ignorance, of life about you both, which I cannot understand.'

Kirkdale laughed gaily. 'The rule of contraries always does surprise people.'

Lady Kirkdale looked hard at her son; he smiled pleasantly; then she said, 'You will never appreciate the difficulties of my position, Kirkdale.'

'Yes, I do, mother, although I may be stupid about obvious truths everybody else appreciates at once; I have a sort of brain of my own concealed in my skull. Geraldine and I were both born old, and we're growing young by degrees, don't you see?'

'My dear boy, what nonsense you talk!'

'Every one must have a childhood some time or other on their own account. In our old home, when my father was alive, childhood was impossible. Let us enjoy it now.'

'Enjoy it, certainly. But bring this new man to see me.' Kirkdale agreed, and Lady Kirkdale sent a note to her old friend John Clausen asking him to come and meet Mr. Travers. John Clausen was a man of vast experience. He had never married, and romantic people told a romantic story of an early love ending tragically in eternal fidelity. He was a walking peerage and encyclopedia; he could tell you the cast of every theatrical success, and the scandals about all the ephemeral celebrities, that have come under the notice of society, and passed thence into the darkness of the outer world during the last forty years. As Lady Maisy Potter, one of Lady Kirkdale's married daughters, said—

'He is one of those charming observant people, who always listen to what you say, and notice what you wear.'

As he sat in Lady Kirkdale's drawing-room on this particular hot June afternoon, he was both listening and observing. Lady Geraldine looked like a fair and sweet flower as she sang Gounod's passionate love-song, *Ce que je suis sans tot*. She was a blonde, with tiny hands which melted in the touch as it were; they appeared to have no strength, no bone, they were so soft, so delicate. Yet now she was playing, you could see they were full of nervous tension; and her style had a certain vigour and distinction surprising to those who had only seen her in her idle moments. Mr. Clausen's eyes wandered from her to the figure of George Travers: he was of light build, his face was clean shaven save for a moustache several shades lighter than his hair, his eyes were brown and rather close together, his nostrils delicate, and his chin well cut. There was a suggestion of cat-like agility about him, and good solid muscle at the corners of his mouth gave evidence that he was a man of endless resource. He stood behind Lady Geraldine, his hand resting on her brother's shoulder. When the song was over, Travers said, 'I should like to hear you singing to a mandolin on the lawn, down at my place at Old Windsor. Can you not persuade Lady Kirkdale to bring you down there one day? It is a charming old place, filled with quaint things I have collected from all parts of the world. I am sure it would interest you. What do you say, Stephen, will your mother and sister come with you and see me in my Arcadia?'

'Certainly, old fellow. I didn't know you had a place in the country.'

'Oh, it is not a property, I simply lease it; but it is convenient to have a house of a certain size in which to store one's collections. I am such a wanderer that I often forget I possess even this little *pied-à-terre*!

'I hear you have such exquisite taste in furnishing,' said Lady Geraldine. 'Lord Foreshot was telling me you had superintended the decoration of his chambers in the Albany, and that they are a perfect dream.'

'I fear Lord Foreshot had some ulterior object in view.'

'I don't understand you, Mr. Travers.'

'I am sure of that, quite sure of that,' and Mr. Travers bestowed upon her a fatherly and forgiving smile. Then he advanced to Lady Kirkdale to bid her good-bye and invite her to make arrangements for the expedition to Old

Windsor. A minute or two later they were joined by Kirkdale, who had remained behind talking to Geraldine. The details were arranged, and the expedition fixed for the following Wednesday by Mr. Travers, who said, 'The middle of the week is always best; one can enjoy one's-self in one's own way without being disgusted by seeing too many other people enjoying themselves in theirs.'

He and Kirkdale left the house together.

'My sister does not like you,' said Kirkdale.

'I am most fortunate.'

'How so?'

'The degrees in a woman's favour are, interest, dislike; interest, hate; interest—well, I suppose I may say more interest.'

'Why do you hesitate, old fellow?'

'Lady Geraldine is a woman who wants a special language to express her. Unfortunately for me, I have not learned it yet.'

'It would please her to hear that.'

'Would it? Then tell her,' and Travers gently stroked his moustache as they turned into Piccadilly.

Lady Geraldine left the drawing-room by one door as her brother and George Travers quitted it by the other. So that Lady Kirkdale and Mr. Clausen were left *téte-a-téte*. She turned to him and said, 'What is your opinion of this man?'

'He is the sort of danger Stephen is bound to encounter sooner or later. The sooner it is over the better; young men must be initiated personally into the mysteries of life, no mother can bear the tests for them.'

'You are quite right there; but I could have wished the serpent of Stephen's choice had taken another form.'

'There I disagree with you; if you had had a free hand in the matter I don't think you could have chosen better.'

Lady Geraldine re-entered; her mother made room for her beside her on the sofa, and said, 'We were talking of Mr. Travers; what do you think of him?'

'I dislike him, and told Stephen I did so; there is an uncomfortable feeling that you are walking on very thin ice when you are talking to him. I wish we had not arranged this visit to Old Windsor.'

'Shall we write and put him off? We had other engagements for the day; I can easily make excuses.'

'Oh no, we had better go. The country air will be pleasant in any case.'

'And how are you getting through your first season, Lady Geraldine?' said Mr. Clausen.

'I feel as if I had been through it again and again before. It interested me at first; it was amusing to see my sisters' old experiences renewing themselves as my turn came. But it is terrible to think that whether you are in it or not, the world goes on just the same: in another season, girls now in the schoolroom will be going through the mill exactly in the same way as I am doing. How one longs for something different!'

'Yes we all have felt that. I believe it is the strongest passion of the human race to get at "something different"; it is the secret of all sin, the secret of all progress.'

'And it is the function of society to suppress this tendency,' said Lady Kirkdale. 'It crystallises, I may say sanctifies, the present state of things. "Whatever is, is right" must be the ostensible motto of those who would retain their places in it .It is the solid edifice round which an empire is gathered.'

'The solid centre of a very wobbling circumference,' interrupted Mr. Clausen.

'Mr. Travers was saying that the beautiful was only a veil to cover the ridiculous. It seems to me that in the same way the stupidity of society is concealed by hiding it behind very high walls,' murmured Geraldine, as she leaned her head on the broad back of the Chesterfield sofa.

'There you are wrong; those high walls contain everything. There is nothing without that is not within; the only difference is that people in society keep within bounds, others do not.'

'That is a great deal to be thankful for,' said Lady Kirkdale. 'I once had to go down to Richmond by the last underground train from Hampstead on a Saturday night. I have had a good deal of experience, but never have I witnessed such a pandemonium. I would not enter one of those underground stations, when the rabble is at large, to save a hundred pounds.'

'All vice loses its attraction when it is seen from the outside,' said Mr. Clausen.

'Has vice any attraction?' asked Geraldine.

'Not to the refined or cultivated pleasure-seeker, but the crude youngster often finds himself thoroughly enjoying the most vulgar vices: it is only after being repeatedly shocked at the appearance of other people when they are enjoying similar ecstasies that our cultivated perceptions render us incapable of revelling in the ridiculous.'

'Ah, how true! nothing excites virtue so much as the spectacle of other people's vices,' said Lady Kirkdale.

'It is the last rope thrown out by Providence to save us from our sins,' replied Mr. Clausen.

'How curious it would be,' said Geraldine, 'if the next Saviour of the world should be one who would bestow a universal sense of humour!'

'But nobody is so ridiculous as a humorist,' cried Lady Kirkdale.

'One can forgive anything when it is done with deliberate intent,' was Mr. Clausen's rejoinder, 'but other people's instinctive emotions can never be forgiven, unless we happen to share them.'

'So you think we might be redeemed by a humorist?'

'He certainly should have a trial. Lady

Geraldine, here is a chance for you—start in life as the high priestess of humour.'

'I am not old enough, Mr. Clausen; I am afraid I have not worn out my instinctive emotions yet.'

'Ah, well! when you have, you will know where to fly for refuge.'

Lady Kirkdale sighed, and said, 'I suppose our most lasting delusion is that our experiences can be of service to others.'

'It is not a delusion,' replied Mr. Clausen warmly. 'Experience teaches us through our own agony to sympathise with others. When they have passed through a like experience, we can help to heal their wounds; but we cannot prevent them fighting out the battle for themselves.' He stopped suddenly, walked to the window, looked out, and said in a lighter tone to Geraldine, 'And how are all your sisters?'

'They are very well. Mary has just taken the new baby into the country, where her husband joins her as soon as the session is over. Emily is still working in the East End; she lectures at Toynbee Hall on Temperance next Friday. Gladys writes from the Embassy at Vienna that her life is wasted in writing official notes; and Maisy and her husband seem to have disappeared altogether ever since they were married; they were most ridiculously attached to each other, as no doubt you remember. All the while they were engaged, I was afraid of stirring about the house, and got into a habit of humming, coughing, and rattling door handles, which I have not overcome yet.'

'And where were they when you last heard of them?'

'Well, they remained in Egypt on their honeymoon, until it became too hot to hold them, and now they've taken refuge in a yacht.'

'Dear! dear! dear! who would have thought so much romance was left in the world? How long have they been married?'

'Six months.'

'The other day I heard it said that the first six months of married life were the most miserable in a woman's existence. Maisy would not agree with that.'

'I suppose not; they utterly refused to return to London for the season, although mamma begged Maisy to come and take me about. Poor mamma, how tired you must be of chaperoning us!'

'No, I am not. As age comes over one, one begins to take an interest in details quite incomprehensible to the young.'

The door opened, and the footman announced in a loud voice, 'Mr. Potter and Lady Maisy Potter.'

'Mamma!'

'Maisy!'

'Robert! Where have you come from?'

'Landed at Portsmouth this morning. Thought we would take you by surprise.'

The reunited family settled itself into groups, more tea was ordered, and confidences exchanged.

Maisy, pert, pretty, and blooming with health, sat between her mother and sister on the sofa. Mr. Clausen and Robert foregathered at the other end of the room. Geraldine said, 'Last time you wrote, you said nothing would induce you to return to England yet.'

'That was all poor dear Robert; he begged and prayed me to stay out there with him, until I really had to threaten him.'

'My dear Maisy!'

'Yes, mamma, I positively had to threaten

him that, if he persisted in staying I should come home alone.'

'And that brought him round at once, of course,' said Geraldine.

'Oh yes, he can't bear me to be out of his sight for a moment. People tell me his devotion positively makes him ridiculous.'

'You don't mind that, I suppose.'

'Geraldine, what has come over you? What is the matter with her, mamma? Has she been crossed in love?'

'My dear Maisy, why should you think so?'

'There's something so nasty, and hard, and cynical about her—positively there is, mamma; one always notices these changes when one first comes home more than people who are living in the house.'

'I don't expect you noticed me at all before you went away.'

'Oh yes, I did; you were always most interested about my affairs, and anxious to know how Robert had behaved, and what he had said. And I know very well you never spoke in that tone then. You hurt my feelings, Geraldine. I'm not used to cynicism. Robert is so straightforward and manly, he never makes fun of me.'

'I wasn't making fun, I assure you; I think you the most enviable woman in the world; really I do.'

Maisy aggrievedly allowed herself to be kissed, and peace was restored. In the meantime, Mr. Clausen was discussing the subject of his return with Mr. Robert Potter. Clausen began by making the remark, that the last news had led him to believe that they had not proposed returning to England yet. Mr. Potter led Mr. Clausen into the recess of the window and said: 'The truth is, my wife was most anxious to remain out there. Personally, I hate missing a season; it is like losing sight of a generation in the evolution of the race, one is always looking for the missing link; and the next year one is horribly out of it. However, I got my wife to believe that this was her own feeling, and after two months of delicate manoeuvring, I induced her to persuade me to return to England.'

'I congratulate you on your patience.'

'A capacity for patience is the bulwark alike of the solid Englishman and of the British Constitution. The principle of the Government has always been to acknowledge such and such a move to be a good one, but to take no step in the matter until it is forced upon it from the outside. It endures. I shall endure. What is the use of having such a splendid public constitution if you do not model your own constitution upon it?'

Mr. Clausen laughed; Mr. Potter smiled. They turned away from the window and joined the ladies.

In a miserable little garret in a small street off the Strand, a young woman lay tossing and turning in her bed; sometimes a little moan escaped her, then she would bury her face in her pillow and break into passionate sobs. As it became light she got up and looked out of the window; she could see a wide expanse of roofs, and in the distant sky the thin lines of white light through the grey river mist. She shuddered at the cold, and crept into bed again. Just as she was falling asleep, a man in evening dress and a loose overcoat of the latest fashion softly entered the room, and she sprang up, saying—

'O my George, my dear one, where have you been? I was terrified.'

'My poor little child, all is well, don't cry: there, there! I have done great things tonight, and if you are very careful our fortune's made. To-morrow we go down to the place on the river Guaschaci has lent us; but my little wife will have to be very obedient, and do exactly what her husband tells her. Does she promise not to cry any more, and not to spoil her pretty eyes?' He held her face between his hands, and kissed her on the mouth.

'Yes, yes, George, anything. I will do anything you tell me, only promise me never to leave me again like this. It makes me so unhappy.'

'My darling, I never will; but you should trust me.'

She threw her arms round his neck passionately, 'I do, George, I do. God knows what will become of me if I ever lose that trust.'

'My sweet love!' and he sat down on the bed. 'Now tell me. Do you remember the simple little cotton dress you wore when I first saw you on the stage, and when you stole my heart from me all at once, before I had time to realise my danger?

Do you remember it?'

'Yes, George, of course I do, of course I do.'

'Well, what do you think I have in my head?'

'I can't think. O George! are you going to let me go back on the stage, and earn money to keep you out of this miserable poverty?'

'Pooh! child, what would five pounds a week be to a man like me? That's no good. No, now listen. In this world the only way to make money is to be supposed to have money. If I can really get the position which is mine by right, and from which my cursed ill-luck cut me off six years ago, when that affair about the duel with Prince Blank, I told you about, came out, the world will be at my feet: I shall be in a position which will be unassailable, because it will be founded on a rock. My exile has been useful to me in this way, it has enabled me to find out secrets which will be invaluable to me; secrets which will make me feared by the leaders of society.'

'O George, but that sounds dreadful!'

'My Gracie knows her husband would disdain to use the knowledge in his possession. Of all blackguards the blackmailer is the lowest. But there are certainly delicate means of working things, called wire-pulling in diplomatic circles, which have a certain charm—a sensation between that of a spider weaving its web and the pleasure of exercising skill experienced by the consummate chess-player. This is a feeling not ignoble; it is one shared by all great statesmen. It is the exercise of this power that evolved the Conqueror of Europe from the Corsican soldier. My wife must learn that all success is the result of carefully adjusted combinations. She must learn to know that to help her husband, and herself, she must exercise inviolable secrecy and enduring self-control.'

'O George, can I help you? Will you trust me? Oh, how happy, how happy you make me!'

'You can and shall; but at first secretly, and in a way which would make an ordinary woman quail.'

'I can endure anything, anything for you. Only tell me, you shall see. I seemed so useless in your real life; it seemed as if I wasn't really necessary to you; now I shall be the happiest woman in the world.'

'Well, I'll tell you my plan. When I go down to Windsor, I want you to live in the little cottage belonging to The Oaks, and to save you from scandal you must pretend to be a poor relation of Guaschaci's. You shall have a little girl to wait on you; no real hard work. Then at night, when the house is locked up and the servants are gone to bed, I shall steal down to you and we will adorn you with silks and jewels and lace, and you shall be my beautiful transformed bride.'

'But, dearest, why?'

'For two reasons. One is that, to work my present plans, I must not be supposed to be married, least of all must I be supposed to have married an actress; and the second is, that that foolish boy whom you met me walking with the other day has never forgotten you. He is constantly asking who you were. I said you came from the country, so that he will not be surprised to find you down at Windsor when he comes next week. He is quite a boy, and very easy to manage. It will lead to no unpleasantness for you, my dearest, or you know I should not propose it. He is the Marquis of Kirkdale, only twenty-one, and by means of his family, who are in the best set, I propose to get really into the swim; once there, the rest is easy.'

'I thought we should have such a lovely time down there, boating and lying about on the lawn; and all the servants to wait on us.'

'It would have been ideal, but, under the circumstances, what am I to do? I must either make my fortune in society, or out of it. I am not born to be poor; I have no talent for it. In society all things are possible, out of it all things are possible; but out of society diplomacy is called lying; statesmanship, cheating; gallantry, seduction; a fine taste in champagne, drunkenness. No, Gracie, you must not ask me to give up society. I am made for it, and it for me. Besides, am I not providing you with the means of gratifying your taste for acting?'

'But what will the servants think?'

'A gentleman's servants know that their first duty is not to think,' said Travers, kissing her.

'Dear George,' she murmured, 'I am a nasty, bad-tempered creature. I have always been teasing you to let me go back to the stage, and after all this will be great fun, and I shall have the leading part at last!'

'Yes, the leading part, Gracie. The other women will only be walking ladies. They will come on, speak a few words to explain the plot, and be seen no more.'

'Who are the other ladies, George?'

'Only Kirkdale's mother and sister, Lady Kirkdale and Lady Geraldine Fitzjustin. They are coming down with him on Wednesday; but if you play your cards properly he will find The Oaks sufficiently attractive to come down without them in future.'

'George, do you think it is quite right, all this deception? Wouldn't it be better to say you were married, but your wife would never, never interfere with you?'

'Dear little baby-wife, no. Don't you see what fun we 're all going to have? Women never have scruples about anything on their own account, but they are always full of them when they think their husbands are risking the purity of their moral characters.'

'Now you are laughing at me, George, but really—'

'No more buts. I'm dead tired,' and he yawned as he turned out the light.

'He is a delightful man,' said Lady Kirkdale, as she leaned back in the corner of the railway carriage after making a charming bow to George Travers, who stood on the platform watching their departure from Datchet station. 'And the house is a perfect gem of exquisite taste.'

'He is much nicer than I thought at first,' said Geraldine. ' It was too bad of you, Stephen, to stay behind, and let him do all the work. Punting two women about must be most wearisome.'

'I fancy Travers likes punting; he knows he has a good figure. I didn't want to spoil the effect,' rejoined Stephen.

'That's the first time I've heard you speak a word against him,' said Lady Kirkdale.

'One stands up for a fellow as long as he's being abused by one's people, of course, but when they begin to appreciate him one can slack off a little.'

'What is the matter with you, Stephen?'

'Oh, nothing—I'm tired, that's all.'

In the meantime George Travers rebalanced the dogcart, fondled the horse, lighted a cigar, and drove slowly back to The Oaks. It certainly had been a successful day for him. His was one of those natures which delighted in gorgeous dreams. He felt realities to be most inadequate, he hated them. Just as he had mounted the winged steed of his imagination, some dirty little fact was always seizing the reins, and dragging him down to earth; but to-day everything had gone smoothly.

His father had been a successful actor in the 'sixties, named Swanwick. Now there are two kinds of bad parents: the parent who looks upon a child as a machine capable of perfect rectitude if its moral principles are manufactured on a certain plan, and the parent whose only notion of a child is that it is a sort of toy sent by Providence for his amusement. Now it amused old Swanwick to see his little son imitating the manners behind the footlights, lounging at bars, patronising pretty girls, advising them as to their costumes, for the actresses soon discovered that it pleased his father to see him taken notice of, and pleasing old Swanwick went a long way towards success. It made all the difference between the smooth and the seamy side of theatrical life. Blind admiration for him, and his, was all that was necessary; but woe to any one who suggested an alteration in his arrangements. He would turn on his most favoured fair one the moment she overstepped the bounds with which his vanity entrenched him, saying, 'Am I the stage manager of this theatre or are you, madam?' This outburst would be followed by language unfit for publication, and days of sullen anger, the clouds only departing after the most complete self-humiliation of the offending one. Now old Swanwick loved his profession; he loved trotting along the Strand and turning in to 'have a drink' with all the cronies he met in his progress. He also loved racing. Whenever, by hook or by crook, he could escape rehearsals, which were much less intermittent in those days than now, off he would go with his friend Travers, to Newmarket, Epsom, San-down, anywhere. Driving for choice, and making a day of it, getting back to the theatre in a state of robust hilarity, putting his head in a basin of cold water, and coming out 'fresh as a daisy,' as he put it—at any rate capable of giving a capital performance of the tender, good-hearted fellow he delighted in portraying. When he died, his friend Travers adopted the little orphan boy. He was a man of old family, and felt the necessity, which old Swanwick had ignored, of doing something more for the boy than sending him to a day-school. Accordingly he talked seriously to the small precocious person whom he had taken under his protection; told him he intended to make him his heir, and that to learn to keep up his position he must acquire some knowledge of the life led in the world on this side of the footlights. He spoke in a way which appealed to the lively imagination of the boy; and when he had stayed for a few months with Travers in his house in Piccadilly, and had been taken down to the place in Gloucestershire for the shooting season, he was completely prepared to ignore his previous experiences; and could treat them lightly as the excursions of a gentleman's son into Bohemia. Travers got very fond of the boy as time went on, and by the time he was thirteen made up his mind to do his very best for him. He sent him to Harrow and afterwards to Oxford, but the City of Spires was rather too much for young Travers, as he was everywhere called now, and he was sent down after one term.

However, he had got all he thought necessary out of the university. He could talk about it, and that was all *he* wanted. He then was put in a crack regiment; but unfortunately for him, he had not been there a year before his patron unexpectedly died, having made no will, and George Travers was thrown on the world with very little but a thorough knowledge of the ropes, some talent for backing the right horse, and a very considerable talent for winning at poker; and it was not a duel but a card scandal that brought his early career in London society to an untimely end. He was obliged to leave England, although circumstances necessitated the hushing up of the scandal. He joined a theatrical company in America, and made a somewhat substantial success out there. He returned to England with some money and the intention of continuing his stage career under his father's name. While waiting for a chance, unaccountably to himself, he fell in love with Grace Lovell; we all have our moments of weakness, and in one of these he married this child, who was full of dreams, full of ambition, full of hopes, wild as only those of a young actress who has made her first success can be. She had been engaged as understudy for one of London's favourite soubrettes, had been called upon to play the part at a moment's notice. She had done so with such dainty freshness, and had made her points with such innocent piquancy, that she had attracted public notice to a Very considerable extent. She played the part three weeks, and during those weeks George Travers came to the theatre, saw, and conquered. When her engagement was over she married him at a registry office, and disappeared from the stage. As fate would have it, almost the moment he had taken this step George Travers made the acquaintance of Lord Kirkdale at the Junior Carlton, whither he had been taken by Charles Melton, an owner of racehorses. The two got on very well; the next day they lunched together, and, strolling along Pall Mall afterwards, encountered Mrs. George Travers. She looked at them expectantly; George smiled, nodded, and gave her a little sign to pass on without speaking. She did so, but not before Kirkdale's curiosity had been vividly aroused. However, Travers vouchsafed no information, but that she lived in the country and he supposed she was up in town shopping for the day.

A week or two later, just as he was changing

his last fiver, he encountered an Italian, Count Guaschaci, whose life he had saved in a taproom free fight, out in the Western States. Guaschaci listened to his troubles sympathetically, and as he was leaving England for six months, told him he should be really obliged if he would look after his establishment at Old Windsor; all he asked of him was to keep things going until his return.

Then Travers saw his opportunity had come. Ten years had passed since the old scandal. A new generation ruled; all was forgotten, or could be explained away. The trustful Count gave him a cheque for two hundred pounds, and left all his affairs in his hands. It must be noted here that Travers had many most endearing qualities. He could not bear to see animals suffer; he got on splendidly with children. He treated women as if he was their father, and men as if he was their redeemer. He took a favour as if he were bestowing a benediction. He had discovered the art of living upon other people with as much grace as if he belonged to the highest circles; none of the bourgeois arrogance of the parvenu or the middleman was perceptible; he took other people's money, their property, and their affections, with equal grace and admirable cordiality.

Grace peeped timidly out of her cottage door as he drove by. He whispered, 'All right, little woman, I will be over directly.' Then he drove the cart into the stable-yard, threw the reins to the groom, and strolled into the house through the back way, calling out as he passed the kitchen, 'Just bring me a whisky and Seltzer in the grey-room; I shall want nothing more to-night'

He lighted another cigar and threw himself full length on the white bear-skin which covered the canopied divan at the upper end of the room. The walls were hung with dull grey material, and decorated with strips and borders of faded Eastern embroidery. Guaschaci certainly knew how to do things well. There was not another man in England for whose decorations Travers felt he could have brought himself to take the responsibility. Certainly this place positively did even him credit; he felt no hesitation whatever in saying that it was his own. A middle-aged woman brought in the whisky, then courtesying gravely she asked if the master would speak to her little boy, he cried to see the master before he went to bed. 'Bring him in, certainly, bring him in.'

'I put him to bed, sir; but I can't get him to sleep; perhaps you will excuse me bringing him down in his little dressing-gown.'

'Certainly, I'll put him to sleep in no time; don't you trouble, Madame Kudner.'

The housekeeper went and fetched her little boy. As she carried him in he held out his arms to Travers, who lay back on the white divan laughing gaily.

'Want a romp, little man?' he cried. 'All right, you shall have one. It is a shame. I haven't seen him all day. Come and look in the cupboard, and see if we can find anything nice there.'

And the boy, who was a miracle of baby prettiness, with little brown curls dancing round his rosy cheeks, and bright eyes, was carried off in triumph to the old oak chest in which the stores were kept.

'There, figs won't hurt him, will they, Madame Kudner? Now, we'll take in the dish; come along. Why, you've got no shoes on! Well, jump upon my back,' and he raced round the room with the child, carrying the piece of massive church plate which did duty for a dessert dish in their curious establishment

Little Pierre sat gravely in the corner of the divan with his feet stretched out straight in front of him, munching the green figs and gazing with rapture at the purple lusciousness which each fresh bite discovered. Travers promised to bring him upstairs when he appeared sleepy, and soon the whole house was still.

The two had a long serious conversation, and Pierre was instructed in full detail how to make himself a little paper punt, which he was to float down the river next evening with a wax taper in it; it was to be saturated with oil, so that when the taper had burnt down the whole boat would flare up splendidly and go down the stream like a real burning ship. Just as this exciting point was reached, a gentle tap was heard outside the window.

Travers listened for a moment, then he hurried off his *protégé*, popped him down on his bed, told him he must go to sleep at once, kissed him on both cheeks, and ran downstairs. He opened the verandah windows, at which the taps had become more and more persistent.

Grace entered in a loose white dress.

'Why have you come here? I told you not to on any account.'

Grace stopped short, it was the first time he had spoken to her in that hard voice.

'You said you were coming down to the cottage. I saw all the servants' lights put out here. I was tired of waiting.'

'I was playing with Pierre.'

'Pierre, at this time of night! You prefer anything to me; even a child.'

'Even a child! That's good. Children are the only perfectly satisfactory companions in the world. They never seriously reproach you, and as for beauty, no woman can touch them.'

'George, let me go away. Let me go back to London, to my old life.'

'I tell you once for all, I can't allow my wife to go on the stage.'

'It is too hard, too hard. You make life a perfect torture to me. Why won't you let me try to forget you, and my love, my unhappy love for you?' she sobbed.

'Don't be ridiculous; and for Heaven's sake don't make such a row. How do I make you miserable?'

'I wouldn't mind if I never saw you at all. When you were quite away at Boulogne the other day, I could set to work at things I wanted to do quite happily; but when I know you are near me, and I am hoping to see you come in at any moment, my hope tortures me. They say hope is a pleasant feeling, I think it is the keenest form of torture the devil ever dressed up as an angel. I sit there in that cottage and wait, and as time goes on all my love turns sick; I get to hate you for causing me such pain. I feel as if I could kill you sometimes, to put an end to it, once for all.'

'Oh dear! oh dear! How absurd, how absolutely ridiculous all this is! If you had just come out of the schoolroom I could have understood it, but any woman who has led the life you have must surely have grasped a few of the elementary realities of life. You appear to think what people say on the stage is real life, and what you see behind the scenes is playacting.'

'So it is. Behind the scenes of a theatre nobody is the same as they are in their own homes; we all play our parts there, but we put all the reality we have in us into our acting.'

'Silly child! I am saying the absurd notions you have about love appear to have come out of plays. Of course, people always say beforehand that eternity will not be long enough for their raptures. The curtain falls on this situation; if it was to rise again, they would have to own ignominiously that half an hour had been found ample.'

'My God! and I believed you when you told me you could not live without me. In six weeks I see you flirting with another woman.'

'Oh, is that it? Well, I suppose if I had cared to play the spy, I should have seen you flirting with another man.'

'How dare you! how dare you speak like that, when you know you asked me to be your decoy! You needn't deny it; that is the long and short of it, and I refuse, I will not submit to this. I will go away, and you can get a divorce if you like. The whole thing is a miserable, degrading, horrible dream. Now I am awake, and will escape.' She rushed to the door; he reached it first, and caught her in his arms.

'I never saw you look so beautiful.' He covered

her face with kisses. She struggled; he murmured, 'My own dear love, I was only teasing; don't let us remember a word we have said.'

'But you were flirting with that Lady Geraldine!'

'Never mind her; she is the sort of woman men always imagine they are in love with, except when they are alone with her.'

'When were you alone with her?'

'I haven't been alone with her, but I can read women like books; you needn't be afraid that curiosity about the sex will lead me astray.'

'And you really meant it when you said I was the only woman you ever really loved?'

'You know it well enough, my darling. When a man like me marries, he has been shot straight through the heart.'

After a pause, she said, 'Well, shall we go back to the cottage?'

'No, we'll stay here and have a little feast. Come along, we will forage about and get up a bottle of champagne. You get the things out of this cupboard, while I go down to the cellar.'

❦

The next morning Grace Travers woke up rather earlier than usual. The scene of the previous evening had left a distinct memory behind, although it had ended in a reconciliation. She had exchanged a few sentences with Lord Kirkdale, and there was an air of truth, candour, and unsophistication that appealed strongly to her imagination, as a contrast to her husband's somewhat brutal analysis of sexual relations. A civilised woman has very little taste for what may be termed pure passion; it pleases her instinct perhaps, but it revolts her intellect, her imagination, her delicacy, her pride. To an intellectual person the whole business of love-making is ridiculous, and without dignity. Dreams and fancies are invoked to give it an adventitious interest, and so a sort of mesmerism is exercised, and blissful dreams of eternal happiness come into existence, depending for their duration very-much upon the sympathy between the imaginations of the lovers, which sometimes is powerful enough to build up a reality from a vision. However this may be, when love comes in at the door intellect flies out of the window or sleeps the sleep of the disgusted.

When it returns to its habitation it delivers stern judgment on the follies that have been committed in its absence. Now a lovers' quarrel interferes considerably with the glamour of the situation, it disturbs the harmony which is essential to the conditions described, and the intellect takes the chance to slip in and give an opinion. So it happened to Grace. She was clever, and before the madness came over her (for in her case it was not a sympathetic imagination which attracted her) was considered witty and brilliant. But the first effect of her love was to make her take life very, very seriously; she became quite incapable, for a time, of seeing the humour of any situation. She had hitherto led a wild roving life, and her ideal had been to settle down in a little nest of her own and play Joan to George Travers's Darby for the rest of her life. Now Travers did not particularly object to her playing Joan, but he did find himself unequal to the combined *rôles* of Romeo and Darby. Romance and domesticity are not a very suitable combination, and poor Travers may perhaps be forgiven for falling short of the ideal set before him.

As has been said by a lady who has made some

study of the female heart: 'What is really necessary to a woman's happiness is two husbands, one for everyday and one for Sundays.' She really meant that she has discovered that Romeo and Darby cannot be combined in one poor mortal man, so is willing to take them separately. Grace was not so reasonable. The romantic attachment she had formed for Romeo, in the person of Travers, prevented her enduring the presence of Darby, in the person of Kirkdale. She did not object to Darby's homage, but it was certainly not worth thinking of, and would certainly meet with no reward from her hands.

All the same, she was conscious that a potential Darby was looming in the horizon, that she was not the woman to waste her life at the beck and call of a man who could talk to her as Romeo had last night. As all this was passing through her mind her eyes fell on an old bookshelf, on which various dusty old volumes were heaped. She walked over to the corner, wondering she had not noticed them before, and took one down: it was a book of plays. She stood reading to herself and laughed, then she replaced the volume and opened a book of Shelley's poetry.

She opened it at the last pages of a play and softly murmured the words to herself. By degrees she read louder, something about her voice struck her. She listened, it sounded different, a new beauty had come into it. She read on and on, wondering at the pathos of the tones she uttered, almost crying with sympathy. As she listened to the laments of Beatrice di Cenci, it seemed to her some inspired spirit had entered her body and was making use of her voice to reveal to her what life, and love, and divine sorrow meant.

From that day she settled down to hard work. She heard that some of the words, as she spoke them, sounded round and full, and moved her to the depths of her heart; others sounded little and thin, and she resolved to work away until she had got all alike resonantly beautiful. Often she caught an ugly jarring sound in her voice when calling out to her little maid, and at once corrected herself. However she was occupied, she kept the one idea before her of making every sound she uttered beautiful.

On Saturday night Travers brought down Lord Kirkdale to stay till Monday. Grace went to church, and was listening to the curate's reading with a severely critical ear when she became aware that Kirkdale had entered the building. He overtook her as she was crossing the fields on her way home. He raised his hat, and said—

'So you are still here? I thought you would have left long ago, you seemed so terribly bored last time I had the pleasure of seeing you.'

'Yes, I 'm still here.'

'And still bored?'

'No; I 'm not bored now.'

'How is that?'

'I am studying something.'

'What?'

'Well, I suppose you'd laugh at a country girl like me if I told you, but I'm studying because I want to go back—I mean—I want to go on the stage.'

'I think it would be a very good idea.'

'Do you really? Oh, how nice it is to hear some one say that!'

'Why, don't you get any encouragement from your people?'

'No, I don't.'

'Look here! can I help you in any way? I might perhaps be able to; I sometimes meet actors and fellows who know a lot about the stage.'

'Oh, thanks. I don't think I want help—yet. But it is most kind of you to offer. I dare say I shall get a chance some day.'

'But I 've always heard you can't learn acting off the stage. You can't do much by yourself down here surely?'

'You can't learn to *act*, but you can learn to *speak* beautifully; life teaches you that, more than all the theatres in the world.'

He looked at her in surprise.

'I don't know, of course, but that's my idea of things,' she said smiling.

'And how do you study?'

'I learn parts, and say them over and over again to myself until I get just the sound I want into my voice.'

'What parts? Juliet?'

'Well, Beatrice in *The Cenci* is the one I like best I don't like Juliet; all that sort of sentiment is such a delusion, you know. I can't pretend to believe in it; but there is a real, terrible tragedy in Beatrice, you can't help feeling it; it takes hold of you, you can't escape it.'

'*The Cenci* is very improper, isn't it?'

'I dare say; I just read the play through once to understand the part of Beatrice, I forget about the details. I only know the fact that she has a real, terrible wrong done her, which makes her loathe herself and lose her wits for a while, that she revenges it, and is beheaded for her crime just as life had become possible for her, when the father that had poisoned the very air in which she grew up had ceased to live. It seems to me that is the only really tragic part ever written for a woman. Lady Macbeth was a fiend, Juliet a baby.'

'Will you read some of it to me?'

'No. I can't bear reading in a room, it is so amateurish.'

'But just quietly, to one person, surely that is different'

'Well, perhaps I will. No, I'll tell you what; if you like to come down to the river mead, I will bring out the book and read a little of it this afternoon. Now go; I don't want the girl to see us come in together.' He obediently went on ahead. She sat on a stile for a moment or two thinking. 'Suppose I go off; suppose I get an engagement, what then?' Lord Kirkdale looked round as he turned the corner, which took him out of her sight. And she wondered why he looked so heavy and sheepish, and foolish.

In case my reader should get a wrong impression of Lord Kirkdale, they must be here informed that he was an extremely well made young man, six feet one in height, thirteen stone in weight, with fair hair and ruddy complexion; there was nothing comic or unseemly about his appearance, but to a woman who had taken it into her head to adore the type of man represented by the Dancing Faun, no Hercules, however laboriously devoted, need apply. '

'Who is this dreadful ineligible man Robert tells me was dining here the other night?' said Maisy. She had been lunching at Davies Street with her mother and sister, and the three were sitting in the drawing-room.

'I don't think you need trouble about his being detrimental, unless it is on mamma's account; he devotes himself entirely to her,' said Geraldine.

Lady Kirkdale laughed. 'I was telling Geraldine the other day, that in a few seasons no woman this side of fifty will have a chance in society.'

'I wonder what the meaning of it is,' said Maisy.

'Age has its advantages,' said Lady Kirkdale. 'Besides, as Edgar Allen Poe says, "What man truly loves in woman is her womanhood."'

'That's so true, dear mamma; a womanly woman can do anything she likes with a man, the other sort sets his teeth on edge at once.'

'A womanly woman indeed,' broke out Geraldine; 'it is only within the last few years women have dared show their womanhood. At last they are permitted to possess a small quota of human nature; they may be something more than waxen masks of doll-like acquiescence without disgracing themselves in the eyes of the world.'

'My dear Geraldine, don't be so disgustingly Ibsenish.'

'You make me perfectly wild, Maisy. Do you suppose all these questions haven't been working in everybody's mind for the last fifty years. You may be pretty sure they have, if we have come to hear of them. I consider the whole machinery of society to be especially contrived to keep an influential set of people sufficiently ignorant to effectually counterbalance the work of men and women of genius, who see clearly enough what the next stage of progress will be; and the mob would follow them readily if the dead weight of authority and influence did not keep them back.'

'Mamma, what is becoming of her? My dear Geraldine, you'll never get married if you go on like this. You'11 have to take to lecturing on temperance or something, like poor Emily.'

'I hate marriage; I think it's a degrading bargain, which can only be carried out by unlimited lying on both sides.'

'Really, mamma; why don't you speak to her?'

'Because I can't deny the truth of what she says.'

'But—look at Robert and me!'

'Yes, look at you, that's just what I mean—'

'Geraldine, my dear, my dear, hush!' cried Lady Kirkdale. 'You mustn't talk like this, you distress Maisy. And after all, you needn't be so bitter about it. God knows, if you prefer not to marry, I am not the woman to wish to force you to it. You've been upset, hadn't you better go and lie down?'

'Oh no! I'm all right. One must speak sometimes, one can't spend one's life grinning like a Cheshire cat, and pretending one thinks everything perfect.'

'Well, to change this very unpleasant subject,' said Maisy, 'what is this Mr. George Travers like?'

'He is tall and slight, I should say about forty, with a careworn face and a charming smile: he can dance, ride, scull, and play billiards to perfection. There is no subject on which he is not well informed,—in fact, if he were only safely married, he would be a great acquisition to society,' replied Lady Kirkdale.

'And Geraldine is in love with him,' said Maisy.

'How dare you say such things!' cried Geraldine.

'When a girl, who is generally good-tempered, becomes snappish and disagreeable, you may be sure she is in love with a detrimental. The detrimental is on the spot, you are snappish.

The situation is complete, my dear.'

Geraldine walked out of the room and banged the door loudly.

'What is to be done about her, mamma?'

'I must take her abroad, I suppose. Love is like bronchitis, a thorough change is the only cure.'

At this moment Mr. Travers was announced.

'I must apologise for this untimely call; but I have just been at the club, and Lord Snordenham was mentioning that he must send round to tell you that his coach had to start half an hour earlier for Hurlingham tomorrow than was arranged. I said I should be passing your door, and he commissioned me to deliver the message.'

'Thank you very much. You are to be one of us, then?'

'I have that honour.'

'May I introduce you to my daughter, Lady Maisy Potter. She has just returned from her honeymoon.'

'O mamma, don't give such a wrong impression! I must tell you, Mr. Travers, my honeymoon lasted six months,' she said, turning to him with an engaging smile.

'It ought to last for ever,' he said, bowing. 'At anyrate it has agreed with you splendidly.'

'Oh, please don't say that; I know I am terribly sunburnt. It is so dreadful to come to London looking so healthy, late in the season, isn't it?

'I am afraid my tastes are not sufficiently aesthetic to allow me to appreciate a sickly style of beauty.'

'I am so glad to hear you say that. It is exactly what I think myself; only it doesn't do nowadays to say anything you think, or one might be taken for one of those dreadful advanced people that are always clamouring for free thought, and free speech, and free everything. I feel it so very necessary to keep on thinking just what is right and proper. Our responsibilities as leaders of thought are so grave. For we are the leaders of thought, are we not, Mr. Travers?'

'After a certain point necessarily so. Progress is made in circles; and if you stand still long enough you will find yourself in the van.'

'But,' said Lady Kirkdale, 'suppose it doesn't come back to the same point exactly, but goes onward in a spiral.'

'That's the whole problem of life. Is it a circle

or a spiral?' said Travers.

'If it's the latter I am sorry for all of us.'

'Oh, don't be afraid, mamma, life is very nice as it is. We'll take it for granted it's a circle, and sit still and not bother ourselves. Spirals are such uncomfortable-looking things.'

The carriage was announced, and Lady Kirkdale asked Travers to drive with them. He did so, sitting next to Geraldine and opposite Maisy. They dropped Maisy at the hotel in Albemarle Street she and Mr. Potter were staying at. Travers of course escorted her in, and as they parted she hoped he would accept the invitation to come to Cowes that her husband was going to send him for the yacht-week.

When he re-entered the carriage he said to Lady Geraldine, 'I imagined your sisters were all out of town.'

'So they were when we last spoke of them, but Maisy and Mr. Potter returned last month.'

'Ah, I met Mr. Potter at your dinner-party on Thursday, of course. I didn't know he was a relation.'

'He is an odd man. He has inherited a large fortune from his father. He is what I call disgustingly rich; he never seems to do anything with his money. His chief pleasure in life seems to be sitting still and thinking.'

'What does he think about?'

'Nobody knows. I used to offer him a penny for his thoughts last year, but he always made one answer.'

'What was that?'

'He only said, "My mind is a perfect blank."'

'Oh,' cried Lady Kirkdale, 'that is like those Indian people who sit contemplating their big toes all day. What are they called?'

'Do you mean the Yogis?'

'Ah yes, that was it.'

'I am never quite accurate about things. You see, Geraldine, dear, it's one of my womanly qualities.'

'Are you going down to Cowes, Mr. Travers? I think I heard Maisy asking you to join her party.'

'Are you going?'

'We have taken rooms in the hotel.'

'Then I shall certainly take advantage of the proposal. That is, if Mr. Potter sends the invitation. Does his mind ever cease to be a blank?'

'No one knows.'

It was the first Sunday in August Lady Kirkdale and Lady Geraldine Fitzjustin had gone to spend a few days in Essex with Mary, the eldest daughter of the family, before proceeding to Cowes. Lord Kirkdale, left in possession at Davies Street, had invited Travers to dinner, and the two men were sitting in the smoking-room ruminating over their cigars and whisky and Seltzer. There had been a long pause in the conversation when Kirkdale suddenly looked up and said, 'Look here, Travers, who is this girl down at the cottage?'

'I 've been waiting for that question for some time; I thought she must have told you herself.'

'Not a word.'

'Well, I think perhaps I ought to let you know that she is secretly married to a very dear friend of mine.'

'Ah, I knew it; she is your wife.'

'Ha! ha! ha! that's good; my dear fellow, you never made such a mistake in your life. I may be foolish, but I'm not such a fool as to go and put my head into a noose like that'

'Travers, I don't believe you. I am sure she loves you.'

'That's quite possible.'

'Look here, you think you're a very clever man; you think you are deceiving the whole world, because you can deceive a parcel of women. But the time has come for a little plain-speaking, old fellow. I know all about you. Clausen has told me. He recognised you that first day you called in Davies Street. He was present when the card-party at Canning's ended your career in London society. Since then I have had many proofs of how a fellow can go from bad to worse; how a man who begins with cheating at cards can end by picking up half-crowns from his friend's dressing-table. No! no! old fellow, hitting me won't put it right,' and he seized Travers by the wrists.

'What are you going to do?' said Travers, helpless and sullen in Kirkdale's powerful grasp.

'I am going to hear the truth about this girl.'

'And what else?'

'Then I shall decide what to do. Who is she?'

'My wife, you fool! Now are you satisfied?'

Kirkdale dropped his hands suddenly. Travers

walked over to the looking-glass, settled his cuffs, and wiped his forehead. Then he leaned his back against the mantel-piece and surveyed Kirkdale, who had thrown himself into an armchair on the other side of the room. After a pause he spoke.

'I need not tell you, Kirkdale, that I have long foreseen this situation: I knew we should have to come to an understanding sooner or later.'

'And you played your cards accordingly?'

'There is no necessity to be so bitter about it. When a man has absolutely nothing but his wits to rely upon, he must cultivate them.

Because I have acquired some skill in the marshalling of events, I don't see that you need reproach me. We all have our temptations. Your father succumbed to the temptations of idleness, I to the temptations of necessity. I was brought up rather more luxuriously than yourself, for my father's vices did not make him bad-tempered; your father's did, and that always has a chastening effect upon a man's offspring. As I was saying, no want of mine was denied until I was practically cast on my own resources, just at the age when one's tastes are most expensive. I needn't tell you what it means to be in a crack regiment with no private income. I had not learnt how to make money as a middleman, or by gambling on the stock exchange; the only resources open to me I took advantage of and kept afloat for some time, then luck deserted me and the crash came. I went abroad; I associated with men not fit to black my boots. My life was a perfect hell. My God! how do you suppose a man brought up as I have been can earn enough to keep him going in a way that makes life worth living? One must have at least five thousand a year. Where is it to come from?'

'Oh, go to the devil!'

'Precisely, that is the only answer to my question. I have been.'

Kirkdale rose and walked up and down the room impatiently. He snapped his fingers.

'I don't care that for you. I am thinking of her.'

'I don't think that is at all a proper way to talk to a man about his wife, my dear boy.'

'Oh, damn!'

'By all means.'

Kirkdale walked towards Travers, who looked him straight in the face. After a prolonged stare they both burst out laughing.

'O what fools we are! what fools we are!' cried Kirkdale almost hysterically, as he flung himself into a chair.

'Well, that's agreed; now let's clear the ground before us. You are in love with my wife; I am as much in love with her myself as the holy estate of matrimony will permit a man to be. She is in love with me, and not with you, unless I am very much deceived.'

'Yes, yes. I had no hope of that kind. I don't know if you can understand or not, but I would do anything on earth to save her pain and to make her life happy.'

'The feeling does you honour, my dear boy. It is one often roused by unrequited affection. A woman who does not love you is always an angel, a woman who does is often a devil.'

'Look here, Travers, don't keep her down in that wretched hole any longer. Let her go on the stage.'

'I can't do that, old fellow.'

'Why not?'

'I know too much about it. The stage isn't a fit place for a woman unless she is a firstrate actress; she must be able to boss the show or quit.'

'But she could boss the show, she'd be first-rate.'

'Not quite that, old fellow. I first saw her on the stage; I could see all she had in her at a glance; it wasn't good enough.'

'She has been on the stage, then?'

'Yes; you may have heard of her, there was some talk of her early in the year. Grace Lovell was her name.'

'I do vaguely remember hearing something or other about her.'

'How long was she on the stage before you met her?'

'Five or six years, I think. She has been working hard down in the country.'

'What at?'

'Oh, reading things. I know I heard her read a bit of Shelley, which fetched me more than anything I 've ever heard on the stage.'

'Well, I'll see what we can do—with her.'

'You may rely on me, if you want help.'

'Thanks, old fellow.'

'And in the meantime?'

'We shall meet at Cowes on Monday. By-the-bye, can I be of any use to you?' and Kirkdale took out his pocket-book.

'Well, old man, if you like to make it a pony this time it would be rather a weight off my mind.'

Kirkdale handed over some notes. Travers took them, folded them up deliberately, buttoned his coat, took up his hat and stick, and walked out of the room. He nodded pleasantly to Kirkdale as he closed the door after him.

Kirkdale sat still for some time, then he lighted a cigar and began to smoke. As he was finishing it the footman tapped and asked if he was at home to Mr. Clausen. Kirkdale signified that he would see him, and Mr. Clausen was shown up.

'Stephen, my boy,' he said, 'this must be put a stop to. I have just come round from the club, and that fellow Travers came in and is hand in glove with every one. Potter was there, and they are sitting down to icarti. You know what it will end in—there will be a devil of a row.'

'I can't help it, old fellow; I have tied my hands in the matter. I must let things take their course. It won't hurt Robert if he does lose his money.'

'But, my dear fellow, we can't possibly countenance this sort of thing. A man must draw the line somewhere, and I draw it at conniving at—'

'It's no use, I tell you. He must be left alone; at any rate, for the present'

'Well, if nothing else will move you, I suppose I shall have to tell you what I really fear from him. He will marry your sister—'

' Oh no, he won't.'

'You don't know her as well as I do. She is a woman who will have her own way, whatever it costs.'

'He cannot marry her.'

'It is what he has been working for the whole time.'

'You're a fool!' yelled Stephen. 'No, no, no! I dare say you're right I've been thinking about something else. I dare say he's capable of it. But I tell you she's quite safe. He is already married.'

'And therefore you consider she is quite safe.'

'She is my sister, sir.'

'And your father's daughter.'

'You will drive me wild between you all,' cried Stephen.

'My dear boy, it's for your own sake.'

'All the damnable things done under heaven are done for my sake it would seem.'

'Have you no regard for duty? Would you like to see your sister fall a victim to this swindler?'

'She must be told he is married, of course.'

'And that he is a low cad no gentleman would associate with.'

'Yes, Clausen, yes, anything you like— anything you like. Be off with you and tell her all you told me and all I have told you. Be off now, no time like the present.'

'Stop a bit! not so fast, my young friend. I want a little more explanation from you first. You say he is married. Where does he conceal his wife?'

'She is at Old Windsor.'

'You have made several excursions there lately. What is she like?'

'Oh, young and pretty; much too good for him.'

'Too vague, my boy, describe her.'

'I don't know how to describe her.'

'Well, is she dark or fair, tall or short?'

'She's dark. No though, her hair is black

and curly, and her eyes are brown, but she has a most beautifully fair complexion. As you sit and watch her reading, you wonder which is the whitest, the little bit of neck shown behind her ear, or the white lawn stuff she ties round her throat.'

'Is she tall?'

'About a head shorter than I am; I suppose that is tallish for a woman. Yes, she's tall, and very, very graceful. She walks beautifully, makes you remember all the old bits of poetry you learned at school.'

'How does he treat her?'

'I don't know.'

'How's that? '

'I have never seen them together.'

'But—'

'She lives at the cottage, he at the house.'

'He isn't married to her.'

'Oh yes, he is; I made him confess.'

'What was she?'

'An actress.'

'No good, of course.'

'Why?'

'He'd be making money out of her if she

were.'

'Her name was Grace Lovell.'

'What! that little girl? Why, she's got the makings of a great actress in her. How comes he to be so shortsighted as to let her remain idle?'

'He tells me she's not good enough.'

'Much he knows! Why, she's delicious; so fresh, so spontaneous. She'd take the town in no time. How old is she?'

'About twenty or twenty-one.'

'Well, to think that rascal has got hold of her. I was wondering only the other day what had become of her, and I asked Horsham what made him part with her. He said she had insisted on leaving, and he fancied she'd gone abroad with some man,'

'I wish to God she had! Anything would be better for her than being tied to such a devil as that' Then Kirkdale asked suddenly, 'By the way, didn't you say Travers was the son of that old rascal Swanwick?'

'Ah yes, capital actor he was; we don't see that sort of thing now. He knew his business thoroughly, and did it. No high-falutin about intellect, imagination, and rubbish of that sort.

He had the instinct here'—and Mr. Clausen thumped his chest,— 'and let the new school say what they like, that's the place to find the link between an actor and his audience.'

'That girl has it *there* too, if ever woman had,' murmured Kirkdale dreamily. 'You should hear her read Shelley.'

'Shelley, nonsense! she's a comedy actress. No doubt she has the touch of pathos necessary for that line; but no power, no passion.'

'She may have altered since you saw her, she's very young.'

'Yes, that's possible. It happened in the case of Décles. You sometimes do get a surprise from a woman in that way.'

'Now, Clausen, like a good fellow, think over what's to be done. I am determined to get her back on the stage. Shall I take a theatre for her?'

'What nonsense! As things are at present, you might just as well chuck your capital into the gutter. She won't draw until she's done a good deal more hard work, and if you gave him such an opportunity, Travers would spend your money for you and she'd get none of the benefit.'

'No, the first step is evidently to get rid of

Travers.'

'That is very easily done. I have only to say what I know.'

'I wonder if he has anything up his sleeve: he's always vaguely hinting that certain personages are at his mercy,' said Kirkdale.

'Very likely he has a whole bundle of scurrilous gossip at his finger-ends; but after all it doesn't very much matter, people say all they can now, and no respectable paper gives currency to these things. Such stories serve two purposes: they give the radicals something to talk about, and add considerably to the popular interest. "One touch of nature makes the whole world kin," and the poor sinner in the street feels his heart go out to the weaknesses of the great, in a way never to be invoked by the mere pompous exterior of public ceremonial.'

'But think of the effect on public opinion.'

'My dear boy, when Burke said a country was ruled by its public opinion, he was right. The only difficulty about it is that the real public opinion is never expressed; what is expressed is what each man or woman thinks his or her neighbours consider ought to be his or her opinion. But to return to Grace Lovell; what do you suppose she would do if her husband was sent back into limbo?'

'I'm terribly afraid she 'd go with him.'

'Have you ever discussed the position with her?'

'She does not even know I am aware of the marriage, she has kept her own counsel; all she has said to me was, that she was anxious to go on the stage.'

'Let's go down and find out about her. I want a little country air, and have nothing on earth to do on Monday.'

'I was going down to Cowes, but I'm sick of the function there; if I go down on Tuesday or Wednesday I shall see all I want,' said Kirkdale.

'Agreed; well, I'll be off. Find out the best train, and call for me in the morning.'

A loud knock at the front door delayed Clausen's contemplated departure. He looked at his watch and said, 'By Jove, it's two o'clock! We'd better open the door, the servants will be in bed.'

Potter was standing on the doorstep. He entered, and said, 'Sorry to disturb you, but it's rather important I should see you at once, Kirkdale.'

Clausen offered to go. Potter stopped him, saying, 'It doesn't signify. It'll be all over the place to-morrow. Only I thought I owed it to Kirkdale here to warn him.'

'Well, come in; sit down and have a smoke.'

'I don't mind if I do; I want to settle myself a little. To tell the truth, we've had a hell of a row.'

'Ah!' said Kirkdale, feeling his blood run cold, 'it's all out, then?'

'What, you knew? And you allowed such a man to associate with your mother and sisters. You must be mad.'

'Yes, I suppose I am. What has occurred?'

'I suspected Travers, from the first time I saw him. Then Maisy came home charmed with him. You'll pardon my saying so, but I always regard that as a bad sign; I find she has a natural affinity for rogues.'

Clausen chuckled.

'I admit it I am no exception. I am no doubt a rogue myself, but that doesn't make me inclined to tolerate other rogues. I met this Travers at the club two or three times, and I noticed him playing at cards. To-night I proposed a game of *écarté*, and gave him a good chance for his particular little game. I caught him in the very act, and, as I have said, there was a devil of a row.'

'What has become of him?'

'Well, after we had made it sufficiently clear to him that we did not desire more love and knowledge of him, he went out into the void. I followed shortly after and came here, thinking he possibly might have come to give you his version of the affair, and there might be another chance of wigs on the green. My blood's up now. That's the worst of a nature like mine. Just as I get thoroughly roused and interested everything is over. And my blood has to simmer down again in a desolation of peace and good humour.'

'He hasn't been here. But I'll tell you what, Potter, I'd have given a thousand pounds not to have had this happen to-night.'

'I'm very sorry, Kirkdale, but next time you propose to bring a cardsharper and blackguard into your family circle you had better take us into your confidence, so that we can have some common basis of operations. Good night, Clausen. Good night, Stephen. Better luck next time, eh!'

Grace Lovell was lying asleep when a hansom cab drove up. Travers opened the door of the cottage with a latch-key, and bursting into her room told her to give him a couple of sovereigns without delay. She scrambled up, opened her little desk, and produced the money. He paid his cab, then came in, sat down heavily on the side of the bed, and breathed hard for a moment or two. Suddenly he fell forward on the floor. She sprang to his side, wetted his face, loosened his collar, held smelling salts to his nose, but for a long time it seemed to her his heart had altogether ceased to beat. Presently he moved slightly, and she renewed her efforts to revive him, calling him by all the endearing terms she could think of. At last he put out his arm and held her gently against him, whispering that she was his darling wife. She nestled close to him and kept perfectly still, waiting for him to speak. After a long time he opened his eyes and sat up; she begged him to lie down on the bed, which he did, but it was some time before he spoke. Then he said, 'It's all up, Gracie, I 'm a ruined man. I shall have to go away.'

'What has happened, my dearest?'

'They have done for me between them. You know I told you that I knew a good deal more than some people would like to set about; well, they came to hear of it, and they have made use of one of their agents, a despicable man, to ruin me in the eyes of society. He induced me to play *écarté* with him; he manipulated the cards in such a way that I should appear to be cheating; then he denounced me before the whole club, and they believed him. I had to go.'

'O George, why didn't you turn the tables on him, and tell them what he had done?'

'My dear child, it's no use a woman supposing she can understand these things; you must take what I tell you on trust; don't keep making idiotic suggestions, and asking idiotic questions. I tell you it was so, that should be enough for you.'

'Yes, George. What are you going to do?'

'God knows.'

'George.'

'Yes.'

'Are you sure you didn't do it?'

'Didn't what?'

'Didn't cheat.'

'Of course not, of course not! Oh, do go to sleep. I've talked until I'm wearied out. I shall go up to the house now.'

'Are you well enough?'

'Don't bother,' and he went out banging the door after him. He lay in bed all day on Monday. About five o'clock he ordered some tea, and played with little Pierre, then he got up and dined. He did not go down to the cottage until about ten o'clock. He found Grace busily engaged packing up. He lounged in, and said, 'What *are* you doing?'

'I am going up to London.'

'What for?'

'I am going back to Horsham's Theatre.'

'No, you are not'

'Yes, I am.'

'How dare you speak to me like this?'

'Because I dare speak to any one like this, when I do not love them.'

'Oh! oh! that's it, is it? We'll see,' and he came towards her threateningly.

She stood perfectly still, looking straight into his eyes. He dropped his hands and sat down, saying sneeringly, 'I always thought women were brutes, now I see it's perfectly true.'

'Yes,' she said, 'women are brutes. If you had loved me, if you had believed in me, and trusted me last night, nothing would have made me leave you. I should not have cared if you had been a thief, or a murderer perhaps.' Here he interrupted her.

'Oh, don't let us have all these heroics. I know it all: you'd go to hell for me, wouldn't you, as long as I feed your insatiable passion for admiration? I'm sick of women and their melodramas.' She stood still looking at him. 'I'll just tell you the plain facts of the case,' he continued more calmly. 'Our love was of that resistless kind, brought about when the appetite is so strong that every other faculty, all prudence, all considerations of every sort, are thrust on one side to gratify it. I admit it is a very charming state of things for the parties concerned, while it lasts, but it does not last long. Our delirium is over. You are a woman full of dreams and imaginations; you worry me with the persistent foolishness of your ideas and ideals. I am a man who knows all the moves, and the long and short of it is that I know how to play the game; you do not.'

'I shall soon learn, and perhaps my game will not be such a losing one as yours has been.'

'No one can tell, but the game is over sooner or later, and then it doesn't matter much whether you have lost or won, the pleasure is in the game itself.'

'Perhaps it does matter.'

'I don't think so. What really matters is letting your chessmen rule you, that is what all mediocre people do.'

'Why have you never talked seriously to me before?'

'Because you were in love with me.'

'What a horribly unscrupulous wretch you are!'

'In his relations with women a man has to act two parts: at first he must be Adam, young, ardent, and resistless, then he must be the serpent, able to teach her all wisdom of the world.'

'And is neither part a serious one?'

'That depends upon the woman. Now we'll talk things over quietly. You want to go back to

Horsham's Theatre?'

'Yes.'

'But it's no use your going on as you used to do.'

'No. I know I was very bad, but I think I shall be better now.'

'Well, let's see what you 've got in you, and then I shall know what is to be done.'

He put her through the balcony scene in *Romeo and Juliet*, making her cry with his severity, torturing her, and finding fault in every possible way with her efforts to express the feeling of the words she uttered At the end of it she stood hopeless and dumfoundered at the new world opening before her. For the first time it dawned on her what acting really meant. She looked timidly at Tfavers. He was sitting in a chair watching her doubtfully. He said, 'Yes, that's very good. You work away at that, and we'll do them all yet.'

'You think I can go back to Horsham's Theatre?'

'No, I do not. But I'll tell you what we will do. I'll run you through the States as a star, and then I'll bring you over to England as a new American actress. We'll do them yet'

'But who is to pay?'

'I'll find the money, don't you worry your head about that.'

❦

On the following Tuesday the waiter at the Crown Hotel, Cowes, respectfully informed Lady Kirkdale that Mr. Potter had sent the pinnace of the *Sunflower* to convey their ladyships on board.

'I suppose, as Kirkdale hasn't arrived yet, you and I will have to go by ourselves,' said Lady Kirkdale.'

'It's a very funny thing he should suddenly change his mind and leave us in the lurch like this.'

'Perhaps Mr. Travers will be able to give us some information; he is to be with the Potters to-day, I believe.'

'I thought he would have called on us this morning. I didn't understand, Maisy, that he was to stay on board with them. Don't you think it's rather odd of the Potters to ask him to stay there when Kirkdale hasn't anywhere to go to?'

'A great many things in this life are odd, my dear, and I'm afraid my thinking won't alter them, so I don't trouble my head.'

As Geraldine climbed the side of the yacht she looked in vain for Travers.

'What has happened to everybody?' she said to Maisy the moment she could take her aside.

'Why? what have you heard?' asked Maisy doubtfully.

'Nothing. Kirkdale has not sent a word of explanation. I thought we should get an explanation from Mr. Travers, but he is not here either.'

'Come down to my cabin a minute,' said Maisy, leading the way into an exceedingly shipshape-looking little apartment, full of the typical *multum in parvo* contrivances which have been invented for the convenience of those who have little space at command. They sat down on the locker, and Maisy began—

'A dreadful thing has happened, and I don't know how to break it to mamma, I'm sure.'

'To whom?'

'Of course, I think Kirkdale terribly to

blame for not making sure first—'

'What are you talking of? Is Kirkdale dead?'

'No, no, what nonsense! I mean he should have made sure of Mr. Travers.'

'Good God, Maisy! you will drive me mad. Is Mr. Travers dead? Say yes or no.'

'Perhaps it would be better if he were.'

'Has he had an accident? Is Kirkdale nursing him?'

'I tell you he's quite well. You won't let me explain properly what has happened.'

'Go on,' said Geraldine, in a dull, toneless voice.

'He played a game of *écarté* with Robert at the club on Saturday night, and Robert found out that he was cheating him.'

'What did Robert do?'

'Well, he watched him very carefully, and when he was quite sure he got up and told him he would not play any more with him.'

'Then what happened?'

'The members of the club were very angry, I believe, and agreed that Mr. Travers should not be re-admitted.'

'I think Robert behaved abominably.'

'Why?'

'I think he owed it to Kirkdale to shield his friend. What does it matter whether a man cheats at cards or not? Everybody cheats, at other things besides cards, in their own particular way.'

'My dear Geraldine, how often have I told you we must take things as we find them? It is considered wrong for men to cheat at cards, and it disgraces them. It is not considered very wrong for women to cheat at cards; people rather expect it, and laugh at it. It's no use arguing about it. It is so, and there's an end of it.'

'Why should there be one law for men and another for women?'

'I don't know, I dare say there are some things winked at in a man which would not be permitted to women. I don't know what they are, but one never can tell.'

'What will Mr. Travers do?'

'Disappear.'

'O Maisy, how dreadful! I expect he is terribly hard up. Can't we help him?'

'I expect Kirkdale is seeing after him. Kirkdale is very foolish. It is a great pity he has not turned out better. He is such a very handsome man.'

'I don't think Mr. Travers handsome, if you are talking of him; but there was a sort of pleasure in his society I never felt with any one else.'

'Yes, he had a charm, there is no doubt of that.'

'You think so. You felt it too. O Maisy, Maisy, whatever shall I do?' Lady Geraldine broke down into passionate sobs. 'I am a fool! What shall I do? what shall I do?' she cried.

'My poor dear Gerry, don't cry; I didn't know it was as serious as all this. I took a great fancy to him myself, but I don't feel as badly as you do, thank goodness.'

'I know he is the only man in the world I could ever care for,' sobbed Geraldine.

'Try and think of somebody else.'

'I hate everybody else. If I think of other people, it is only to think of the difference between him and them. He is so graceful, they are so proper. He always has something charming to say, they always say the things one has heard over and over again. He is like the Dancing Faun, they are like a tailor's block. Oh, what is the use of saying all this? He makes my heart beat with happiness when I only hear his footstep. When

I touch other men my blood turns cold, and my heart turns to ice.'

'Geraldine, Geraldine, you are really dread ful. I 'm sure it isn't at all proper to feel like that. I never felt so about Robert. I always liked other people. Of course, one feels that one's husband is one's husband. But still—'

'I never thought I felt like this till to-day I didn't realise it before: it has come upon me suddenly. It is as if I had been swimming about' in beautiful blue water, and suddenly found myself being sucked down by a whirlpool.'

'Don't you think we had better ask mamma about it? I really don't know what to advise.'

'Not on any account. Swear to me you will not breathe a word of this to any one. I shall get over it. Don't be afraid. See now, I will bathe my eyes and come upstairs.'

Geraldine soon effaced all traces of her emo- tion, except a slight redness about the whites of her eyes, and the two sisters went on deck.

Robert Potter had in the meantime communicated the news to Lady Kirkdale, who was sitting under a large Japanese umbrella looking unusually perturbed. Geraldine took her place under the awning and was soon surrounded with a group of merrymakers, and she laughed and talked and picnicked, drank champagne, and made feeble jokes, quite as gaily as the rest. However, directly she got back to the hotel she told her mother her head ached. She went and shut herself up in her room. Here she wrote the following letter:—

'DEAR MR. TRAVERS,—I am so sorry, so very sorry, for what has happened. I have been afraid you were in money difficulties for some time. Will you give me the happiness of helping you out of them? Believe me, you have my deepest sympathy. I don't believe in society, or any of its laws. I enclose twenty-five pounds in notes, hoping you will accept them as a proof that I will do anything I can to extricate you from the difficulties in which you are involved.—Yours always sincerely, GERALDINE FITZJUSTIN.'

She took the letter to the post herself. It was almost the first time in her life she had left the house unattended. She felt that every one must know what she was doing, that she was being watched, and that the post-office clerk guessed the reason of her sending a registered letter. At last she completed the business, and putting the tell-tale little flimsy receipt-paper in her purse, she hurried back to the hotel. Just as she entered it she encountered Lord Kirkdale and Mr. Clausen, who had that moment arrived.

'Out alone, Lady Geraldine?'

'Yes, what is one to do when one's brother deserts one like this?'

'Your maid?'

'Gone out herself; she didn't expect us back so soon, I suppose; we have been on board the *Sunflower* all the afternoon, you know.'

'Have you heard the news?' asked Kirkdale as they entered the private sitting-room.

'Yes; what has become of Mr. Travers? Is he at Old Windsor?'

'He is.'

She sighed with relief.

'Clausen and I went down yesterday and arranged to get his wife something to do.'

'His wife!'

'Oh! didn't you know that he was married? I thought you said you had heard the news.'

'Married? married? When? who to?'

'About three months ago: a most beautiful girl. You may have heard of her—Grace Lovell —she was an actress.'

'I don't remember,' said Geraldine, in a bewildered tone. 'What did you say? Why didn't he tell us?'

'I can't say. It's all very ugly, on the face of it; and I tell you what, Geraldine, I 've come to the conclusion that he's one of the biggest villains on earth. I did you all a terrible wrong in bringing him to the house. I have to ask your forgiveness.'

She looked at her brother a long time, and the tears gathered in her eyes; then she turned away, and hastily entered her own room. Here she found her maid laying out her clothes for the evening.

'Never mind now, Elizabeth, I want to lie down quietly.' As she spoke she crossed to her writing-desk and her eyes fell on a sheet of note-paper on which she had scribbled the first wild words that had come into her head when she sat down to write to George Travers. There they were, staring her in the face,' My dearest, dearest one on earth, I have heard of your ruin. Come and let me see you once more. I will give you all I have to enable you to—'; then she had stopped herself and written the more moderate note for 'his eyes', leaving her real passionate words, the words which had been the expression of her inmost feelings, for the eyes of her maid.

She turned to look at the woman, but found she was calmly taking her wrapper out of the wardrobe. Had she seen or not? No trace was visible on her face. Geraldine sat down in front of the glass, and said, 'You can wash my head, Elizabeth; I think it will refresh me.'

The woman made all the preparations. While she had gone for hot water, Geraldine seized the incriminating note and tore it into a thousand pieces. She had just time to thrust it behind the grate and walk quietly across the room when the maid re-entered. Her eye fell for a moment on the writing-table. 'She has read it,' thought Geraldine. She sat quite still for a long time; then she said, 'What should you say if I were to marry Lord Foreshort after all, Elizabeth?'

Elizabeth started visibly.

'I should hope your ladyship would be very happy, I'm sure.'

'Why were you so surprised?'

'I didn't think your ladyship seemed willing to take him before.'

There was a long pause while her hair was washed, and Elizabeth was rubbing vigorously when Lady Geraldine said, 'How is your poor sister now?'

'The one that was deceived so cruelly?'

'Yes. The one that fell in love with a married man.'

'Well, your ladyship, I didn't like to tell you after all your kindness to her in finding her that place and all, but I'm very much afraid she's gone off to America with him.'

'Really! She has done that, has she?'

'I was afraid your ladyship would be annoyed, so I didn't mention it. But she disappeared, and some time afterwards I had a letter from her, telling me about how he had got a bit of land out in Canada, and she had joined him there.'

'And what were they doing?'

'I'm sorry to say, they seemed doing very well; she wrote most bright and cheerful like. I must beg your ladyship's pardon for saying it, but they do say the wicked flourish like green bay trees, don't they, your ladyship?'

'I suppose they do, sometimes; but don't be sorry they are happy, Elizabeth.'

'No, your ladyship.'

'Elizabeth, I want you to bring all the letters that come for me into my bedroom. Tell the waiter to give them to you.'

'Yes, your ladyship.'

'You'd better have that black silk petticoat; it will be nice and cool for you to wear, and I shall keep to white all the rest of the summer.'

'Yes, your ladyship.'

'Now I will lie down; don't let me be disturbed until it is time to dress for dinner.'

'No, your ladyship.'

'A telegram for your ladyship,' said Elizabeth as Geraldine entered her bedroom about twelve o'clock next morning to get ready for a stroll on the beach.

'All right. I shall not want you for a minute or two.' Elizabeth discreetly left the room.

She opened the brown envelope, took out

the flimsy pink paper, and read, 'Have started for Portsmouth. Will write. Travers.'

That she could not prevent, that she could do nothing to stop, him coming was a thought that filled her with exultation. He was getting nearer and nearer every moment; and what was more, she was to have a letter from him—it would arrive that evening by the last post perhaps; if not, certainly in the morning. Then she thought of his being married, but it made no difference; she knew he had married before he saw her, that was all that really mattered to her. She rang for Elizabeth, and crushing the telegram up put it into the front of her dress. She dressed, and went out in the highest spirits. She was charming to every one, and made herself so agreeable that Lord Foreshort felt quite encouraged. He said, 'How well this climate agrees with you!'

'Doesn't it. It is exactly the sort of place I like: plenty of life about, and at the same time everything is clean, and spick and span.'

'It's perfect. Our tastes are so alike.'

'You are always saying that, Lord Foreshort'

'I am always thinking it, Lady Geraldine.'

'Then you have no time to think about your

tastes?'

'No, I am always thinking of yours.'

'So am I.'

' There, I told you we agreed.'

'Well, that's settled. Now let us talk of something else.'

'When will you begin to let me hope.'

'You are hoping now, are you not?'

'Do you really mean it?'

'Mean what?'

'That I may hope?'

'I can't prevent you hoping, can I?'

'Yes, you know you can.'

'Well, I 've tried to a good many times.'

'But you will give up trying now, won't you? Take another tack.'

'Very well. You have hoped without my permission the whole of the London season; you can hope with my permission during the shooting season, then perhaps you will be sick of hope.'

'Yes, I shall claim my reward then.'

'Ah! that's "another story." We mustn't get on too fast.'

That evening the expected letter arrived. It

ran thus—

'DEAR LADY GERALDINE,—You have restored my belief in the human race. I have indeed received a crushing blow from your brother-in-law, and it is not fitting that I should inform you of the true facts of the case. Honour seals my lips. But although it is forbidden to me to justify myself in your eyes without degrading those who must ever be first in your esteem, your generous letter emboldens me to ask you to believe me, on my bare word, that things are not as they, no doubt, have been represented to you. I am coming to Portsmouth so as to hold myself in readiness to obey any commands you may care to issue to your most devoted adorer,

GEORGE TRAVERS.

Geraldine wondered a good deal over this letter, but all the same she wore it next her heart for four days. She wrote in reply—

'DEAR MR. TRAVERS,—I can't think of any way of seeing you here, but next Monday we go to our place near Ringwood. If you will put up at the village hotel there, I will write and let you know what I can arrange.—Yours most sincerely,   G. F.'

On Sunday she took a long walk with a party of friends. She and Mr. Clausen were ahead. Mr. Clausen knew the island well, and had undertaken to act as pioneer. By degrees she led the conversation to the subject which occupied so many of her thoughts, and Clausen found himself giving her a full account of what had taken place at Old Windsor the previous Monday.

'Kirkdale and I went down to Datchet and drove to Old Windsor: there we found Mrs. Travers occupying a little cottage, pretty enough in its way, but only fit for a labouring man,— the chairs covered and windows hung with white dimity, an old oak settle, and so on. You know the kind of thing.'

'What is she like?'

'An exceedingly pretty, dark, slight woman. She is very young; but she gives you an extraordinary impression of knowing her own mind at moments.'

'What is her version of their life together?'

She spoke of nothing but her great desire to go on the stage again; he has been preventing her doing so, all this time. They appear to have been exceedingly happy together otherwise.'

'Do you believe he really loves her?'

'He must have, I should think; there seems to have been no other reason why he should marry her?'

'He may have liked her at first, but perhaps she is a shallow sort of person. I should think he wanted a very deep nature to sympathise with him.'

'I don't think she is shallow; but you mustn't forget, when you talk of depth of character, the thinnest sheet of gold-leaf is a good deal more valuable than a whole bogful of mud.'

'And is she going back to the stage now?'

' We promised to arrange it for her. Horsham is a great friend of mine. She made her success with him, and he was delighted to hear she was ready to come back again; but now—'

'What?' said Lady Geraldine.

'Well, I fear her husband has found out what a little gold-mine she may become. She wrote to me yesterday, saying he had been coaching her in some leading parts, and proposed touring with her in the States if he can get some capital to start them.'

'But isn't he fearfully hard up now?'

'A man like that is never without resources; if he cannot get money out of men, he can get it out of women.'

'O Mr. Clausen, how dreadful that sounds!'

'Lady Geraldine, I beg your pardon. I should not have said such a thing to you; forgive me.'

'No, Mr. Clausen, I beg of you, don't think I am so absurd; girls hear of all sorts of things nowadays. I want to know what you really think Mr. Travers will do.'

'He will do anything that he thinks most likely to bring in a quick return.'

'But what is his object? His tastes are so fastidious. I cannot imagine his being content to mix with actors and actresses for the rest of his life, they are such flashy, noisy people. Whenever one sees any very disagreeable set at Henley or Lords, one is always told they are actresses.'

'Yes, that is the phrase, of course; still, in justice to the profession, I must say that a great many actresses go about quite as dowdily as the royal family. There is no distinctive badge which can be applied to all the members of the profession.'

'But I cannot imagine Mr. Travers tolerating anything that isn't in the best taste.'

'He no doubt prefers everything about him to be of the best; but as he has effectually cut himself off from it by being twice caught in the act of cheating at cards, he will have to satisfy himself with the second best now.'

'Tell me what is a man's real feeling about this cheating at cards. Why is it the most terrible sin he can commit? It seems to me, from hearing people talk, that it is quite possible to break every one of the commandments without losing a single acquaintance, but directly you commit this particular crime the whole world cuts you.'

'I will explain. You know among the Arabs there is another unwritten law, that you may kill or destroy the property of any man who annoys you; but if you have once eaten salt with him, you must hold your hand, whatever provocation you may receive. All these things are a sign of a bond that exists between certain members of the community. Cards are to the European what salt is to the Arabian. They are the sacred symbol of fidelity; and any man who does not feel this must be cast out.'

'But why? it seems such an arbitrary thing.'

'I can't help that. We have all been brought up to believe that it is a beastly thing to betray our friends; and a man must be regarded as a friend from the moment you sit down to a game of chance with him.'

'Well, 1 don't believe I shall ever understand; but perhaps women have no moral sense.'

'Exactly what I have always said, Lady Geraldine. The only safe place for a woman is under lock and key, and even then you ought to stop up the keyhole with sealing-wax.'

'It is because we are kept under lock and key that we don't care what we do. We feel we are unjustly treated, and that we have a perfect right to cheat, and lie, and prevaricate. It is the only means of retaliation we have. Oh, I wonder if the time will ever come when we shall get fair play.'

'No, it will not; I can tell you that much. No man or woman, from the Queen down to the beggar who spends the night on a doorstep, gets fair play. There isn't a single human being in all the world who hasn't been kept back from doing all he might by other people, or by circumstances of one sort or another. This place is meant for a struggle; and the only way to get through it comfortably is to cultivate a taste for struggling.'

'I 'm sure you know you needn't say that to me, Mr. Clausen.'

'Yes, you struggle a little—too much, in fact; for the secret of all success is to discern the difference between the possible and the impossible. Turn your back on the impossible, and make steadily for the possible.'

'O Mr. Clausen, how wise you sound now! I wish I had been there to see when you were young.'

'I wish you had. You would no doubt have found me quite foolish enough to please you then.'

'And did you turn your back on the impossible?'

'Yes.'

'And are you glad you did?'

'No.'

'Ah, I knew that'

'It is perfectly true, a temptation resisted gives you no pleasure; but that does not prevent a temptation yielded to giving you an inevitable retribution.'

'Oh, that sounds so like a copy-book, I am sure it can't be true.'

'What do you mean?'

'Mr. Clausen, can't you understand what it is when a girl grows up and finds out bit by bit everything she has been taught and told is a pack of lies.'

'But surely your mother—'

'No, no, it isn't my mother; it's the governesses, it's the nurses, it's the silly novels, it's other girls. It makes me shudder when I think what a world of shams I'm living in, and what a sham I am myself.'

'My dear child, I fear I have only one consolation to offer you, and that is, that you would shudder a good deal more if you for one moment saw the truths which underlie these shams.'

'You talk as if the world was a pest-house. Surely we are some of us beautiful; we are not all diseased and horrible.'

'One hears a good deal about the beauty of life; but I am very much afraid you will find in the long run that the beauty of life is like the beauty of a lady's complexion—very fleeting, or else sham.'

'There I have cornered you, Mr. Clausen. There's a beauty about a gypsy's skin which isn't fleeting, and which is very real; and it is beautiful, just because it is exposed to the sun and the rain. In a word, freedom is beauty, and gives beauty.'

'Well, perhaps there's something in what you say; but I don't think you'd find gypsies very satisfactory companions at close quarters.'

'I should like to get a chance of seeing for myself.'

'Take my advice, and don't. I am sure your tastes are too fastidious for such realities as that,' said Mr. Clausen, laughing. Here the rest of the party came up, conversation ceased, and chatter reigned in its stead.

Lady Geraldine's mind was much perturbed by her conversation with Clausen. She doubted

Travers, but felt she must see him, she must get some sort of proof herself. Poor girl! after all her outcry, she was only a very ordinary woman, wrapped up in her own little chaos of emotions and foolish little thoughts. She thought it would be a splendid thing to sacrifice herself for love. Mediocrity was her bugbear, just as it has been the bugbear of thousands of other mediocre people, and she was ready to take the most desperate measures to escape from it. The only way she could think of to show how different she was from the rest of her sex was to cultivate her instincts and let them lead her whither they would. To overcome the world and remain a slave to your own passions has been the ideal of all the splendid failures of history, but she only recognised their splendour, and did not stop to consider their defeat. So, with her mind strung up to a high pitch of romantic passion, Lady Geraldine went to meet Travers in the Kirkdale woods.

She found him leaning against a tree cleaning a horseshoe he had just picked up. His little fox-terrier was running about smelling the rabbit-holes and following trails with a suspicious and preoccupied air, as if he was not quite sure whether these joys were permitted to him or not. He ran forward to see who Geraldine was, and licked her hand; then he hung his head and ran back to his master and sat down by his side. Travers looked up; he had not seen Geraldine approach, and he said, 'So you have actually come to see the last of the poor outcast.'

'Is it the last? Is it true that you are going to America to act?'

He started a little, wondering how this could have come to her knowledge, but recovered himself quickly. 'There seems nothing else left for me to do.'

'But if there was?'

'I would gladly take the alternative.'

'I thought so; I didn't believe you could willingly take up that sort of life.'

'Indeed you are right there. What an angel you are to come here like this! I can't think how I deserved such a thing.'

'I don't know whether you deserve it or not, and I don't care much: I have come because I love you, and because—'

He took the hand she held out to him and

kissed it; she put her other hand round his neck, and he kissed her lips. Then feeling he had done all that was expected of him, he was about to gallantly release her, when he found she was almost fainting in his arms.

'By George, this is serious,' he murmured, and he led her to a felled tree, sat her down on it, and went to look for some water. When he returned he found she was calmer.

He had a little pocket flask with him and had filled the cup with water. She refused to drink, but dipped her finger in it and wiped her forehead. Then he sat down by her side, and she leant on his shoulder and said—

'What shall we do? Will you come away from England with me, or shall we stay here?'

'Whichever you think best; your wishes are my law.'

'Well, I'll tell you exactly how I stand. I have eight hundred pounds a year now, and shall have four hundred pounds a year more when mamma dies. It is settled on me, and they cannot take it from me whatever I do.'

'Ah!' he said, 'in the hands of trustees, I suppose.'

'Yes, that is the worst of it: I cannot touch the capital.'

'But, dear Lady Geraldine, have you ever considered what it would be for two people to try and live on eight hundred pounds a year?'

'I know it would be very difficult, but I am willing to try anything if it will save you from that dreadful life. We could take a flat in Venice or Florence, and you would have to be divorced; then we could be married, and no one would mind in a few years.'

'I am sure you would regret it, if you took such a step.'

'I should never regret it I hate this life in England. We would have a beautiful home, and then we could come to your place at Old Windsor sometimes.'

'That is not my house.'

'Not your house! what do you mean?'

'It belongs to a friend of mine; he asked me to take it'. Travers stopped himself, and for once in his life, by a supreme effort, told the truth. 'I mean he offered to lend it me because he was going away. You don't know what a poor devil I am, Lady Geraldine.'

'Don't call me by that hateful title. And so you have been very, very poor. Why, my wretched little eight hundred pounds a year will seem quite a lot of money to you. I am so glad you know what it is to be poor.'

'I can't deny that poverty and I are old bedfellows, Lady Geraldine; but all the same—'

' Why are you hesitating?'

'Well, it sounds rather ungrateful; but I think I ought to tell you that if my wife and I went to America to-morrow, the very smallest salary I would accept would be one hundred pounds a week between us.'

'But your wife is not a great actress.'

'No. If she were a great actress she would get that sum without having me thrown in; but during my last engagement at Mallock's Theatre I had seventy pounds a week myself.'

'I see; I cannot bribe you high enough. I am sorry to have troubled you to come here to-night'

'I am terribly distressed about the whole business; but I am sure you would be miserable living abroad like that yourself. Think of what it would mean. I have been disgraced publicly; you would be disgraced; we should both be shunned as if we were plague-stricken. I am sure you see things as I do.'

Lady Geraldine got up to walk away. Suddenly she turned and flung herself at Travers's feet, saying: ' Oh, don't let us talk or think about the hateful money! Act if you like, if you find it so profitable, but don't, don't leave England. Cut yourself free from that woman. I will do anything you like. I love you wildly, desperately. I cannot, cannot leave you.'

He gently disengaged her fingers. She rose on her knees and looked him straight in the eyes. Then she cried out—

'You don't love me the least little bit in the world. Why is it? Am I not beautiful enough? Haven't you told me a hundred times I was? O George, George, tell me what is the meaning of it all!'

'It means I love you too well to wish to injure you.'

'Then you do not love me at all. Is it that you love this other woman, this wife of yours?'

'Perhaps; I can't tell what it is.'

'I will sit down quietly by your side now; I won't rave at you any more, don't be afraid.

Tell me exactly what you feel.' She stood for a moment, then put her hand in her pocket, took out her handkerchief, then sat down, holding it in her lap.

'Now tell me, dear one,' and she laid her hand on his arm. He shuddered a little. She noticed it and removed her hand. 'What do you feel about her and me?'

'Well,' he said, 'I think it must be this. When I fell in love with her, I did so in the terrible blind, reckless way that only comes over one once in a lifetime. It is more a nightmare than anything else. I couldn't understand myself at the time, and I can't understand myself now.'

'Oh, you have got over it, then?' she said, leaning towards him.

'Yes, I have got over it. I am sickened of love. But my wife is a clever woman. I believe I can do something with her. She has a most extraordinary talent for acting, and that interests me. I don't suppose there is a man alive, take it all in all, who knows more about the tricks of the trade than I do. These are just what she wants to be taught, and it is interesting to me to see what she'll turn out This feeling has taken the place of love. She is about as tired of love-making as I am, and now we are going to set seriously to work together.'

'But if you are so tired of love, why are you here tonight? Did you think you would get money out of me to go to America with her?'

He laughed a little. 'Well, it does sound absurd now you put it like that, but I suppose I did.'

She was sitting to his right. Her fingers closed on something that had been hidden in her handkerchief; then came the loud report of a pistol, a puff of smoke, a groan from Travers as he fell sideways with a crash in a heap among the brackens.

Lady Geraldine sat perfectly motionless for a moment; then she saw the blood beginning ooze from the wound just over his heart, and she drew her dress carefully on one side. She did not look at his face for about five minutes. She turned round then, and saw his eyes fixed on her with a terrible stare.

'No, I will not suffer for you,' she whispered, as if replying to their silent menace, and she put the pistol into his hand and closed the fingers round it. They would not keep as she placed them. At last she left the thing on the ground by his side, then she walked rapidly away. Before she had got far she remembered the compromising letters she had written: she must go back and get them at any price. She found his pocket-book; she found her three letters in it; she took them, and replaced the pocket-book. Then she went. Just as she was leaving the wood, the fox-terrier, which had been off on a hunting expedition, ran up to her, smelling her dress. She put down her hand to pat its head. It licked off a little spot of blood that soiled her first finger. She tried to speak to it, to tell it to go to its master, but she found her mouth was parched and dry. She could not utter a word. But it went all the same, following the track of her footsteps into the wood.

She went through what would probably occur. He would be found alone with a pistol. She thought of what would happen if the pistol was identified. She had taken it from the gunroom at home; she had thought it would add to the romance of the situation. Two of them had been hanging on the wall; she remembered them all her life. Sometimes her father had allowed her and her sisters to practise with them on Sunday afternoons, much to the scandal of the neighbourhood. Kirkdale would go to look at the body; he would be sure to recognise the pistol. She got into the house unobserved just as the clock struck eleven. First she went up to her bedroom and dusted her shoes; her feet were covered with dust. She took off her stockings and wiped them clean as well as she could without making a mess. Then she went downstairs. She had sent her maid to bed. Nobody seemed to be up except Kirkdale and Clausen, whom she could hear playing billiards as she passed the door. She went down the passage, entered the gun-room, and examined the window. She saw it was accessible from the outside. It was one of the old-fashioned hasp bolts, so she took a rusty pocket-knife she found lying in a forgotten heap of odds and ends and passed it between the crack of the window. She scratched the bolt as best she could to make it appear as if it had been opened from the outside; then she dropped the knife outside the window, closed the door, and went to bed. She lay awake wondering if there was any precaution she had forgotten to take; and when at last she slept, she dreamed that she was a child again, and that her father was alive. He was in one of his rarely affectionate moods, dancing her on his knee and calling her his own dear little girl. He called her mother and sisters and little Stephen to look at her as he stood her upon the table—Mr. Clausen was there too,—and then her father laughed and clapped his hands, and said, 'She's the flower of the flock, she's my very own daughter,' and he rushed at the others and chased them out of the room. Then it seemed to her they were afraid of her as they had been of him. She saw their faces peeping in at the window at her, as if she was a terror to them. She looked at her father for explanation, but he no longer spoke or moved; his face was cold and lifeless, as if formed from damp yellow clay; and she went and touched his fingers, which closed on hers, and she felt she was becoming clay too. The cold crept up her arm; she could not stir hand or foot. Just as the cold reached her heart she woke and tried to scream, but once again she could utter no sound, and lay there motionless. At last the morning came. The horror of the dream had taken all her attention: she thought of nothing else; she felt she must speak of it, yet feared that in some vague way it might betray her. She could not bear to stay in the house waiting. She ordered the pony-carriage, and drove herself over to Lyndhurst, where she found some friends at home. They got her to put up there, and she did not return to Ringwood until dinner-time. Driving home she went over in her mind every possible thing that could happen: they would know the pistol; they would find it was impossible for the gunroom to have been entered from the outside; he would have boasted that he was going to meet her; somebody had seen her in the wood with him. She had gone to her room with a headache at nine o'clock, and asked not to be disturbed; perhaps Elizabeth had brought her something just before going to bed, and had discovered her absence. She imagined herself being driven away handcuffed between two policemen. She went through all the horrors of the last scene of all, when she would go blindfold into eternity. She shuddered terribly, then suddenly remembered the groom was sitting behind her, and was probably taking notes of her behaviour, and that he would be able to give his evidence too. As she drove over the bridge a train was arriving at the station. She pulled up a moment and watched the passengers alight. She saw a girl get out of a carriage and a tall man meeting her, and, leading her tenderly through the station, put her into a closed carriage. She saw that it was Kirkdale. Then she understood everything had been found out, and they had sent for the wife.

She drove into the village, sending the groom into the draper's to get her some riding gloves. The man came out to deliver them to her himself. He looked very serious, and said, 'Terrible news, isn't it, my lady?'

'What is terrible?' she asked. 'I have been away all day.'

'A gentleman found murdered in the woods close to Kirkdale Castle.'

'Murdered!' she cried.

'Well, the police are very reticent; I can't say how it was done, but I know he was shot through the heart.'

'Dear, dear! I must try and find out as quickly as possible,' and she drove off without noticing the man's parting salutation.

'Murdered,' she said over and over to herself. 'After all, they know, they know everything.'

Mr. Clausen met her as she drove up to the principal entrance, and solemnly led her into the library. 'You have heard?' he said.

'Yes. Weyman told me that he had been found dead.'

'George Travers?'

'Yes.'

'He has not been publicly identified yet. How did Weyman know who he was?'

'I don't know, I suppose he heard it somehow.' She looked up nervously. She met Mr. Clausen's eyes looking steadily at hers, and she knew he guessed. After a pause she said, 'Tell me what is known.'

'I will. This morning the footman spoke to Kirkdale after breakfast, and informed him the gun-room had apparently been broken into.' Mr. Clausen laid ever so slight a stress on the word 'apparently.' He continued, 'A careful search was made and nothing was missing but one of a brace of pistols, that had been hanging together over the mantelpiece. I formed my own theory on the matter, and was just about to demonstrate to Kirkdale that it was impossible that the window should have been entered from the outside, when the news of the dead body being found reached us. I therefore refrained from making any remarks, and later in the day, when every one was agog over the conveyance of the body to the parish room, I went outside the gun-room window and tried myself to get into it from the outside. I found it was possible, but very difficult, and I knocked down some plaster, besides disturbing a good deal of dust which I had noticed was quite undisturbed in the morning. I may have done away with some circumstantial evidence, but it is always a satisfaction to try things for one's-self.' Again their eyes met, this time with a fuller understanding than before.

'At the moment Kirkdale and I went at once to the scene of the tragedy, and found poor Travers dead, with his little terrier by his side, shivering and trembling, and refusing to stir; indeed, we had the greatest difficulty to coax it away. While the constable was taking notes, I saw the revolver lying among the ferns close to his hand, but the constable did not; I thought it better not to attract Kirkdale's attention to it at the time, so I let them remove the body without saying a word. I then went back to the gun-room and did what I have told you; and having satisfied myself that the chain of evidence was complete, I went down to the village, and advised the constable to come up and search the scene of the fatality more thoroughly. Kirkdale came too, and it was not long before we found the revolver this time. The sight of the pistol at once reminded Kirkdale of the open window, and without a moment's hesitation he told the constable all he knew. The constable came along, and having pointed out to him the marks of feet outside, the footman having given his evidence, and having wired for Mrs. Travers, whom by the way Lady Kirkdale has most kindly consented to put up, and who arrived about half an hour ago, I watched for you, so as to put you in full possession of the facts of the case.' For the third time their eyes met

'How can I ever thank you?'

'Good God, woman, don't thank me! You owe me nothing. It is for your mother's sake that I have become your accomplice, and that I have taken this burden on myself.' She bent her head. He continued, 'People who sin against human life in this way cannot expect sympathy.

Your punishment is that you are cut off from fellowship with your race; the memory of that murdered man will rise between you and those who guess, and those who do not guess, your guilt.'

'Supposing, after all, others discover that I did it?' she whispered.

'They shall not, they must not! I command you not to betray yourself; it is the least you can do.'

'You needn't be afraid. I dare say you think I am sorry that I did it, but I am not; I am glad. I should be miserable if it had not been done.'

'He would never have done anything so criminal as this.'

'No, he hadn't the courage, but he would have sneaked and lied and shivered through life, taking men's and women's souls and bodies and tearing them to shreds, dragging them down until they could see nothing in life but a struggle for amusement, nothing beyond but a rest from torment. I know I did it from a horrible motive, just to gratify my mad injured pride, to revenge myself on the cur that had turned on me; but all the same it is a good deed done, and I am glad I did it.'

'I do not understand you, Lady Geraldine.'

She got up and walked past him to the door; then she turned and said, 'I am my father's daughter. People like him and me belong to a race apart; we are only mortal clay, while you and mamma, and Maisy and all the rest of you have immortal souls.'

She came towards him once more. 'Oh, don't be afraid, I won't touch you, I won't contaminate you. Yes, I see it plainly now: you all of you have immortal souls, you show it in your lives, don't you?'

It was the day of the funeral. *'Suicide while of unsound mind'* was the verdict brought in by the jury. Lady Geraldine was alone with Mrs. Travers for the first time. They were sitting with books in their hands pretending to read. Both were dressed in black. Both were somewhat restless. Lady Kirkdale had left them in the drawing-room. The funeral had taken place in the little village churchyard early in the morning. There was nothing more to be done. Mrs. Travers was going to London the following day to commence rehearsing for a new piece at Horsham's Theatre. Lady Kirkdale had suggested she must stay with them and rest, but she only thanked her very much, and said she should prefer to set to work at once.

Lady Geraldine sat eyeing her surreptitiously. At last she said—

'You are very fond of your profession, are you not, Mrs. Travers?'

'Indeed I am. I don't know how I should have lived during the last few months if it had not been for the thought of it'

'You were going to America, I heard?'

'Yes; George spoke of doing so.'

'Will you tell me what your real feeling about this is; you seem very calm, and yet—'

'And yet I loved him, you mean.' Lady Geraldine nodded. 'Yes, I loved him; and I suppose if this had happened two months ago I should have gone nearly mad with grief. But a curious change has been taking place during that time. It used to seem as if great floods of emotion came over me, enfolded me, and took possession of me. I had no power to resist them. One day I suddenly found I could, as it were, swim through; I knew what I was doing; I could guide and control myself; I could use the emotion as I pleased.

'Yes, yes; I believe I know what you mean; go on telling me.'

'Well, that is what it comes to. In real life you get an emotion which masters you; in art, in acting, in all works of genius, I suppose, you master an emotion. That is why artists are set apart from the rest of the world; they cannot enjoy the common emotion long, they demand too much from it'

'And do you not regret your loss at all?'

'Oh, we are all human, of course. I loved him, but still I feared him. He made me see things in his way: I had no freedom of judgment. When he was with me I thought he was a splendidly clever person; even when I found out how bad he was, and what terrible things he had done, he only had to make some ridiculous excuse for me to believe every word he said.'

'Don't you think it is a good thing for you that he is dead? Don't you feel that if you had seen much more of him you would have become a thoroughly bad woman?'

'Yes, I do. I sometimes wonder even now if I can get away altogether from his influence. But how did you know this? What made you imagine it?'

'I will tell you exactly why. You know we were quite ignorant that he had a wife until about a fortnight ago. I must confess to you that from the first day I saw him I would have married him at any moment if he had asked me, and given up everything in the world for him. I found out by degrees what he was, and I thought that if it were true, I could not bear that he should live. And now that he is dead I am glad. I feel a weight is off my soul.'

'Yes,' whispered Grace Travers, 'that is just what I feel, a weight is off my soul: to live with him was to be morally contaminated. Almost the last time I talked to him, I remember feeling as if it would be a glorious thing to be a great criminal, and that if you could not rule by fair means, you should rule by foul. George had such a horror of mediocrity.'

'He thought anything better than that, eh?'

'Yes, I believe the only person who could really fascinate him would be some one who could make him suffer terribly.'

'Was there anything that could make him suffer?'

'No, I don't think there was, he always took things so easily. But he didn't want to die; he hated the thought of it I can't think how he ever came to kill himself.'

'Well, it is unfortunate that the only person who could attempt to fascinate him in the way you suggest would be compelled, by the circumstances of the case, to prevent him from showing that he was fascinated.'

'Poor George, what a pity he isn't here! That would have amused him; it is just the sort of thing he would have said himself.'

THE END.